S U S A N   F A I T H

PURPLE PUPPY

ILLUSTRATED BY NAOMI OFFNER

PURPLE
PEOPLE
UNIVERSE·at ONE with the

Some of the proceeds from this book will be donated to charities which benefit children, animals and the environment.

AUTHOR'S ACKNOWLEDGMENTS

It seems like the time has flown since *Purple Love*, *Purple Puppy* and *A Purple Day* were written. Upon the publication of *Purple Puppy*, I find myself more blessed and grateful for my journey. Many people have supported, loved, encouraged and helped me to succeed in the publication of *Purple Puppy*. I am very grateful for following my instinct to wait for the right illustrator, Naomi Offner, who did a beautiful job and brought me to tears with her wonderful artwork that gave life to my story; Rudy Ramos once again provided the calm and support needed in those final pre-press moments while remaining a true professional and a pleasure with whom to work; a special thanks to Bridget, Savannah, and Zoe for their help; I would like to thank the many people who have been by my side during the long days of promoting one book while publishing another: my son, Matthew, who has incredible insight, wisdom and candor which encouraged me to broaden my vision and stay on my path, who has a heart of gold, a certainty of who he is and the blessing to remain a purple person; all of my friends, new and old, who allow me to be "out of the limelight"; all of the wonderful creatures of the Earth, wild and domestic, especially PC and Tyrone (age 9), Akiva (age 2), Pinball (age 21), Squeaky (age 19), Frick and Frack (brothers, age 9) and UM the turtle (age 11); my family who loves me even though I frequently could not take their calls when I was writing/editing – Mama Bear Roz, Papa Bear Al, Baby Bro Bear Brian, Aunt Gail Bear, Uncle Russell and cuzzes Evelyn and Myrna; and, especially my partner, Tami, who worked 16 hour days and never complained, who allowed me to vent while maintaining her smile, who knew when to give me a hug, and mostly, for just being the loving, caring, encouraging, sweet, supportive, talented person who does most of the work and gets little of the credit. Most of all, I thank God for allowing me to find the light within and for keeping me on my journey for my soul's highest purpose. I am blessed.

Purple People Incorporated • P.O. Box 3194 • Sedona, Arizona 86340-3194
(928) 204-6400 • www.purplepeople.com • email: info@purplepeople.com

FIRST IMPRESSION
ISBN 0-9707793-0-5

Library of Congress Catalog Control Number: 2004092483

Art Directed and Production Supervised by Tami A. Pivnick
Production Design by Rudy Ramos
Editing by Matthew Broude (Senior Editor), Evelyn Albu, Myrna Goldstein
The illustrations were painted in the U.S. in watercolor and watercolor pencils
The text type was set in Berkeley
The display type was set in Goudy Old Style
Composed in the United States of America

If you are unable to obtain this book from your local bookseller, you may order directly from the publisher at: www.purplepeople.com or by calling toll-free: 1-866-PURPLE5 (787-7535). We offer quantity discounts. Author Susan Faith is available for inspirational and educational speaking.

Purple People, Purple Person, Purple Lady, Purple Puppy and At One With the Universe are trademarks of Purple People Incorporated.

Purple People™
At One With the Universe™

Printed in Canada on acid-free paper

With love for

Matthew, whose loving heart extends to all living creatures;

Tami who radiates in the presence of our four-legged kids;

PC, Tyrone, Akiva, my purple puppies.
They inspire me, delight me, and leave little room for my feet in bed at night!
Their purple spirits shine by their sharing their home, their hearts and the bed
with my purple cats Pinball, Squeaky, Frick and Frack;

Champ, Fax, Emmy Bear, my purple puppies who are no longer physically here.
Those that have passed will forever remain alive through my wonderful memories
of all the loving moments we shared;

My parents, in special memory of Herbert Louis and Sylvia Ruth Dubbin.
When I was born, Dad picked my Mom and me up at the hospital with a dog in the
car! Dad always shared a kiss or a belly scratch with any dog he met. He and I snuck
more than a few puppies into the house in my purse; Mom lovingly allowed them to
stay and become part of the family. Fluffy, Fifi, Mimi, Tonga, Brandy and Kisses all
shared my youth and my heart. They made my childhood special.

—S.F.

It was time for Helen to go to bed. She had a wonderful day so she was slow to get into her pajamas.

"Helen, it's time for bed. Please hurry!" her Mom pleaded. Helen knew that she needed to be quick because tomorrow was a special day, and she didn't want her Mother to change their plans.

"Mommy, Mommy, please read me the story you wrote about the cute little bunny."

"Alright, Helen, that's a great idea since you're getting your own pet."

As her Mom read the familiar words, Helen's eyes began to droop and her lids closed. Mom had barely read a page before Helen was fast asleep.

Her Mom pulled the covers over her, turned out the light and left Helen to her pleasant dreams.

Helen's day had been busy. It was her last day before she would get to bring home her new puppy. They had gone and picked her beautiful, purple puppy when he was only four weeks old. Now he was nearly ten weeks old.

Tomorrow, he would be coming home to live with Helen and her family.

Helen had waited a long time for the day she would get to bring her purple puppy home. She was so excited about getting a puppy that she frequently pretended to be one.

Now she would be with her puppy and they would actually grow up together.

Purple puppies are very special puppies.
They spread their love wherever they go.

Drifting into a deeper sleep, Helen remembered her fun day. Helen and her sister, Sarah, played for hours with their bunny, Purple Love. They cleaned Purple Love's cage and fed him.

Just before Helen's bedtime, her Mother painted a puppy-dog face on her.

As Helen slept, her painted cheeks sank deeper into her favorite purple pillow.

Helen was a busy little girl with a vivid imagination.
She slept soundly. But somehow, before she went to
bed, she knew that this night would be different.

She rolled over and kicked off her blankets.

Pretty soon Helen was running around her backyard,

barking and screeching with delight.

She had always pretended to be a puppy,

but now she really was one!

Helen ran faster and faster, chasing her tail
until she tumbled over into a ball of delight.

She had a pretty tail, one that was easy
to hold in her mouth as she
twisted to scratch
an itch.

On all fours, Helen quickly scampered to go explore her neighborhood.
Things definitely looked different from this level. Everything was so tempting.

Helen knew her Mother loved her pansies. Mom and she had carefully planted
the seeds and taken special care of them. But that was when Helen was a little girl.
Now that she was a puppy, things were different.

Before Helen could stop herself, she gobbled up all of the yellow pansies
and began eating the purple ones. They were absolutely delicious.

As Helen sat with all four paws in her Mother's prize garden, she really liked the feel of the soft dirt on her tender paw pads.

She decided to dig a few deep holes before she moved on.

The dirt reminded Helen of Susan's garden. Susan lived next door and had just planted a big, new tomato garden. Helen quickly ran toward the fence that separated her from the ripe tomatoes waiting to be eaten.

"Hmmn," Helen thought, "how do I get around this fence? I'm not tall enough to reach the gate without human legs. I know, I'll DIG my way under."

Before you could say SCRAM,
Helen had dug herself right under the fence.

There were so many tomatoes that Helen didn't know where to begin.
There were red ones, yellow ones and lots of green ones. Some were very small and
some were very, very big. Helen tried them all. She liked the little red ones the best.

Unfortunately, the easiest ones for her to reach were the
large green ones so she filled up on those
before journeying on.

Helen realized as she looked up the street and saw all of the trash cans that this really was her lucky night.

She put her head high in the air and sniffed for the best goodies. Nothing too appealing was in her family's trash.

Helen walked and walked until she didn't recognize any of the houses around her. But, she did notice a wonderful smell coming from a trash can.

She stood on her hind legs and tried to reach the top of the trash can. It was no use. She was too small to topple it over.

Helen decided to climb on the boxes next to the trash can to get to the goodies. She slowly and carefully climbed to the top box and stuck her head into the trash can.

WOW!
There was almost a whole turkey just waiting to be eaten!

Helen ate and ate. Then she ate some more.

Just as Helen finished the entire turkey, she saw a chocolate cake toward the bottom of the trash can. She leaned in farther and before she knew it, she toppled off of the box straight into the trash, head first!

The can went crashing to the street with a loud clang.

Helen was inside the trash can, covered with sticky, smelly trash.

Helen was beginning to think that maybe digging deeper for the cake was not such a great idea. Suddenly, she heard a lot of barking and saw house lights go on.

Before Helen could get herself out of the trash can, she saw a large dog with huge teeth heading her way. Helen was only a small puppy and she didn't think she could outrun this huge dog. Besides, her stomach ached from all those tomatoes. Eating all of the turkey didn't help, either.

The gigantic dog was only steps from Helen when she heard, "Princess, come here. Come in this house now!" Princess was quick to respond and turned on her heels and ran back to her house.

Helen thought her troubles were over. After all, this was her lucky night. Even though she had eaten too much and her stomach ached, she had not been attacked by the scary dog.

"Get out of there, you pest," Helen heard as she peered up at an older boy reaching to take her out of the trash can. Helen recognized the boy. His name is Michael and he had visited Helen's family.

This worried Helen because she knew Michael had come to visit her family by car. Helen knew she must be far from her home.

Michael turned and left Helen in the dark. She could barely see her paw in front of her because there were so many clouds in the sky.

Helen began to realize that this was not such a lucky night, after all.

As Helen slowly walked up the street trying to catch a sniff of some familiar scent, she could hear many cars and trucks whirring by on a nearby street. Helen grew more and more frightened. She didn't know where she was or how to get home.

She pulled her pretty tail closer and closer to her body. It was cold now in the damp night air and her puppy coat was not too warm. Her tail was limp. As Helen slowly walked on, her paws shook from fright.

Helen was very tired now. Her paws ached. Her stomach grumbled from all of her dining. She wished for a nice warm bed and her loving mother.

Helen decided it would be best to find some shelter and sleep for a while. She found a small tree, barely large enough to fit behind. The sound of the cars and trucks had grown louder so she knew she should wait for daylight before trying to get home.

Helen lay her head on a small, sharp rock. It hurt. She was very lonely. She was very scared.

Then, it began to rain.

It didn't just rain a little.

It **POURED**.

Helen was **VERY** wet.

She stood to shake herself off and began to howl a little.

"Helen! Helen, honey, you're fine. You must be having a bad dream," Helen's Mother stated reassuringly.

Helen could barely believe her ears. She shook her head and looked down. She thought she would see four paws at the end of four legs. Instead, she saw her legs and arms, and her favorite purple sheets.

"Mommy, Mommy, I'm so glad that I'm safe at home in bed. I dreamed that I was a mischievous puppy and I had wandered off into the dark night."

"You are fine, Helen, and today is a very special day. We are going to pick up your real puppy. But, remember, puppies are a big responsibility and you will need to teach him how to behave so that he is safe."

"Don't worry, Mommy, I know all of the things that my puppy should never do."

"Sarah and I will take him to puppy training and on walks on his leash. We'll play with him in our fenced yard. All of the exercise and toys will keep him from getting bored so he won't dig or tear up your flowers. I know he'll love his crate. I put lots of chew toys in it."

"And, Mom, I think I want to wash off my puppy face. It is fun to pretend that I am a puppy but I would rather be your little girl. I know that it is important to listen to you so that I am always safe."

"I am glad that you are my little girl, too, Helen. I am also happy that you know that I tell you things to keep you safe because I love you."

"Let's go wash your face and pick up your puppy."

BEWARE OF PRINCESS

"O.K. Mom. I love you, too."

PURPLE PUPPY has been a wonderful project from the beginning. At the time I wrote it, I lived in Massachusetts and had neighbors from England. Their two children loved to play in my yard with my four dogs. Going home for "proper tea," to do homework, or to get ready for bed, always provided a huge challenge for Helen, age four, and Michael, age eight. On a beautiful summer evening, Helen romped around my yard on all fours, pretending to be a puppy. Not having a dog of their own made leaving my yard and my pups even harder for Helen and Michael. I promised them that if they obeyed their Mother and did as she asked, I would write them a bedtime story. *Purple Puppy* was born!

I truly feel blessed in my life. I live in a gorgeous area surrounded by miraculous red rocks, meet wonderful people, travel, speak on positive topics and am surrounded by much love. Most importantly, I continue on my healing journey, beginning by loving myself. Prior to becoming an author, I was very ill for eight years. I spent much of that time physically limited. I was not happy because I was constantly in pain. I knew that I needed to find a healing path. On a bright and sunny afternoon, I decided it was time to be happy, healthy and to find the power within my heart, soul, and spirit to soar again. I gave up my career in law. I began to meditate, do yoga and play the West African djembe drum. My energy grew and my physical limitations faded into non-existence.

I realize that my illness served a purpose. It taught me to overcome tremendous obstacles. I learned to view the World from a positive perspective. I know that there are no limits in life. I listen to my inner voice and accept that my purpose in life is to share positive energy and inspirational messages. I am grateful that my words touch both children and adults. It is incredibly heartwarming to receive wonderful responses from people from age three to ninety-three.

My message is one of love and seeing the positive in everything and everyone. If we can dream it, we can live it. You create your reality and when you allow yourself, you will soar. Begin by loving yourself.

I founded Purple People Incorporated with the intention of spreading love and peace throughout the Universe by promoting the concept of equality among all humans and respect for all living creatures. I believe we need to honor our differences and cherish our similarities. When we see each other as purple and honor our uniqueness and individuality, we can create equality.

Why Purple? When I began to meditate, I frequently saw the color purple. Purple is the color of spirituality, royalty and healing. I have come to realize that I am truly my happiest when I wear purple, so I wear it almost exclusively! People frequently comment on my "purpleness."

None of us is the *color* purple. However, we can all be Purple People. A Purple Person spreads love and peace. Wherever Purple People travel, they always carry their most prized possession . . . their smiles. A Purple Person loves all of the Universe's creations and respects and cares for them. They teach their children to value life through the simplest lessons, such as walking around ants instead of stepping on them.

I know that children throughout the World want to be Purple People. Let's work together to raise the next generation as Purple People so that we may all be At One With the Universe.™
I send you much love and light in your life—

SUSAN FAITH

Purple People Incorporated promotes the concept of equality and respect for all living creatures. Educating children about the value of all life can easily be accomplished with the simplest of lessons, walk around the ants, don't step on them! We all occupy the same planet and need to co-exist with nature.

Purple People Incorporated publishes books on a variety of subjects that promote positive, inspirational messages. Part of the proceeds from Purple People Books will be donated to charities including those which benefit children, animals and the environment.

Purple People Incorporated

P.O. Box 3194
Sedona, Arizona 86340-3194
(928) 204-6400
www.purplepeople.com
e-mail: info@purplepeople.com

Coming Soon:
A Purple Day by Susan Faith

Purple People Incorporated believes in proper animal care and pet safety. By walking your dog on a leash, providing a fenced play area and a crate or bed inside your home, your pup will not be exposed to the potential danger of wandering the streets.

AWARD WINNING PUBLISHER
2003 GLYPH Award for Excellence in Publishing:
• Best Children's Book—*Purple Love*
• Best Inspirational, Spiritual Book—*Purple Love*

AWARD WINNING AUTHOR, SUSAN FAITH
Proud recipient of the above awards and
2003 Arizona Literary Contest – Children's Literature, 3rd place.

Please be aware that no animals were harmed in the writing and production of *Purple Puppy*. All of the events in this book are fictitious. However, these events could pose serious harm or fatality to a living dog. According to the Humane Society of the United States, poultry bones can splinter and puncture a dog's digestive tract causing serious injury or death. Equally dangerous, chocolate can be fatal to a dog if consumed in large quantities. Other potential risks of a dog fending for him or herself on the street include being hit by a vehicle or attacked by another dog or wild animal.

Please be responsible and loving animal owners. Be sure to have a collar and identification tag on your dog with current information. If you tattoo or microchip your dog, be certain that the registry knows your accurate contact details. Local humane societies are forced to place for adoption animals that have microchips that do not have the owner's proper phone number or address.

A few other suggestions include spaying or neutering your pet and giving your puppy the best opportunity to succeed as a good citizen by enrolling in obedience classes. A well-trained dog makes a better companion and your time together will be more enjoyable. Although we all would love to adopt that cute little puppy, be sure that you have the time, funds, and appropriate living quarters for the pup when he becomes a full-grown dog.

Puppies require attention, puppy dog food, training, exercise and most of all, patience and love. Dogs are with us for life, we do not rent them for a period of time with the option to dispose of them.

Purple People Incorporated and Susan Faith are not animal care professionals. Any suggestions or comments about appropriate pet care and safety are based upon personal opinion and are made only in the interest of raising awareness. Please do your own research and consult with your animal care provider or veterinarian.